Bunny Bungalow

For Madison Grace Mancini —C. R.

For Emily, happily ever after —N. H.

Library of Congress Cataloging-in-Publication Data
Rylant, Cynthia.
Bunny bungalow/Cynthia Rylant; illustrated by Nancy Hayashi.
p. cm.
Summary: A family of rabbits moves into a cozy bungalow, which they
decorate and make into a perfect bunny home.
ISBN 0-15-201092-0
[1. Rabbits—Fiction. 2. Home—Fiction. 3. Family life—Fiction.
4. Stories in rhyme.]   I. Hayashi, Nancy, ill. II. Title.
PZ8.3.R96Bu 1999
[E]—dc21   97-43707

First edition
F E D C B A

Printed in Singapore

The illustrations in this book were done in watercolor and
Prismacolor pencil on hot press Arches watercolor paper.
The display type was set in Cloister Open Face.
The text type was set in Sabon.
Color separations by United Graphics Pte. Ltd., Singapore
Printed and bound by Tien Wah Press, Singapore
This book was printed on totally chlorine-free Nymolla Matte Art paper.
Production supervision by Stanley Redfern and Pascha Gerlinger
Designed by Judythe Sieck

CYNTHIA RYLANT

Bunny Bungalow

Illustrated by

NANCY HAYASHI

HARCOURT BRACE & COMPANY

San Diego   New York   London

The bunnies found a bungalow,
a cozy bunny home.

They painted it as green as grass,
they made it all their own.

Father carved a weather vane
    (a carrot, don't you know),
To twirl around and whirl around
    in wind and rain and snow.

Mother knitted bunny quilts
for all her babies' beds,

And stitched a few white pillows
for her little babies' heads.

The parlor held a rocking chair,
   so nice for bunny naps,

A big soft couch for poetry,
read in bunny laps.

The children bathed with daisy soap
in silver bunny tubs,

Then wrapped all up in fluffy towels
for Mother Bunny rubs.

They played with bunny baby dolls
all dressed in lacy clothes,

Then picked some cherries off a tree
and squished them with their toes.

The bunnies drank their tea at night
to give them sleepy heads.

Then Father read them stories before
sending them to bed.

The bunnies in their bungalow
    slept tight and still and sound,

Then woke at dawn and listened
to their carrot going round.

The bunnies found a bungalow,
  a perfect bunny home.
They live there still, they always will....